Girls F.C.

Helena Pielichaty (pronounced Pierre-li-hatty)
has written numerous books for children, including
Simone's Letters, which was nominated for the
Carnegie Medal, and the popular After School
Club series. A long-standing Huddersfield Town
supporter, there are few who could write with as
much enthusiasm about girls' football. A local
girls' under 11s team helps with the inspiration
and tactical know-how, but Helena has been
an avid fan of women's football for many years.
It clearly runs in the family: her aunt was in a
women's team in the 1950s and her daughter
has been playing since she was ten (she is now
twenty-four!). Helena lives in Nottinghamshire with
her husband and has two grown-up children.

The Girls FC series

Do Goalkeepers Wear Tiaras?

Can Ponies Take Penalties?

Are All Brothers Foul?

Is An Own Goal Bad?

Who Ate All The Pies?

What's Ukrainian For Football?

What's Ukrainian For Football?

Helena Pielichaty

WALKER
BOOKS

For Rhys Jones

First published 2009 by Walker Books Ltd
87 Vauxhall Walk, London SE11 5HJ

10 9 8 7 6 5 4 3 2 1

Text © 2009 Helena Pielichaty
Cover illustration © 2009 Sonia Leong

The right of Helena Pielichaty to be identified as author
of this work has been asserted by her in accordance with
the Copyright, Designs and Patents Act 1988

This book has been typeset in Helvetica and Handwriter

Printed and bound in Great Britain by Clays Ltd, St Ives plc

British Library Cataloguing in Publication Data:
a catalogue record for this book is available from the British Library

ISBN 978-1-4063-1738-1

www.walker.co.uk

☆ ☆ The Team ☆ ☆

☆ **Megan "Meggo" Fawcett** GOAL

☆ **Petra "Wardy" Ward** DEFENCE

☆ **Lucy "Goose" Skidmore** DEFENCE

☆ **Dylan "Dyl" or "Psycho 1" McNeil** LEFT WING

☆ **Holly "Hols" or "Wonder" Woolcock** DEFENCE

☆ **Veronika "Nika" Kozak** MIDFIELD

☆ **Jenny-Jane "JJ" or "Hoggy" Bayliss** MIDFIELD

☆ **Gemma "Hursty" or "Mod" Hurst** MIDFIELD

☆ **Eve "Akka" Akboh** STRIKER

☆ **Tabinda "Tabby" or "Tabs" Shah** STRIKER/MIDFIELD

☆ **Daisy "Dayz" or "Psycho 2" McNeil** RIGHT WING

☆ **Amy "Minto" or "Lil Posh" Minter** VARIOUS

Official name: Parrs Under 11s, also known as the Parsnips

Ground: Lornton FC, Low Road, Lornton

Capacity: 500

Affiliated to: the Nettie Honeyball Women's League junior division

Sponsors: Sweet Peas Garden Centre, Mowborough

Club colours: red and white; red shirts with white sleeves, white shorts, red socks with white trim

Coach: Hannah Preston

Assistant coach: Katie Regan

☆ ☆ Star Player ☆ ☆

☆ **Age:** 10

☆ **Birthday:** 11 November

☆ **School:** Mowborough Primary

☆ **Position in team:** midfield

☆ **Likes:** pancakes with sugar and lemon

☆ **Dislikes:** when people look at me strangely in the street because I am talking to my parents in Ukrainian

☆ **Supports:** Karpaty Lviv

☆ **Favourite player(s) on team:** Eve and Lucy, because I know them best from school

☆ **Best football moment:** scoring special goals

Veronika "Nika" Kozak

☆ **Match preparation:** I clean my boots

☆ **Have you got a lucky mascot or a ritual you have to do before or after a match?**
Not really.

☆ **What do you do in your spare time?**
I learn English with my family; I MSN my friends from my old school in Ukraine; I help look after my uncle and little sister.

☆ **Favourite book(s):** Riding Icarus by Lily Hyde

☆ **Favourite band(s):** Madonna, Okean Elzy

☆ **Favourite film(s):** I like funny films

☆ **Favourite TV programme(s):** Dr Who

Pre-match Interview

Vitaju! Mene zvaty Nika Kozak.

That's Ukrainian. It means hello,
my name is Nika Kozak. Don't worry,
I am not going to write my whole
story in Ukrainian – though I wish I
could as it would make life easier
for me. I have lived in England for
less than two years so my English is
not perfect. In fact, sometimes it is
maytki (pants)!

OK, I am here to tell you all about
the football tournament I played in
during the summer holidays. I was so
excited because it wasn't like last
summer's tournament, playing teams
from our league and completed in
one day.

This time we were playing girls'
U11s football teams from all over the
country at a place called Sherburn
Sands. We had to sleep over for three

nights and compete for the World Cup.
Yes, the World Cup, no less.

Not everybody from my team could
go. Holly, Amy, Tabinda and the funny
twins, Dylan and Daisy, were all on
vacation. I didn't think I'd be able
to go, either, because each person
had to pay towards the costs and I
knew we didn't have enough money for
things like that. Imagine my delight
then when Hannah, our coach, told me
that there was one free place if I'd
like to have it. "Please say yes," she
said, "or we'll be down to six and
won't be able to go!" Of course I said
yes. And thank you.

So here is my story. May it bring
you peace and happiness.

Lubov,
Nika x

1

I was in my bedroom, or rather, *our* bedroom at my Uncle Stanislav's house where we live now. I had only half an hour to go before being picked up for Sherburn Sands. On my bed in front of me was an untidy heap of things ready to pack. Leaning out of the window behind me was an untidy heap of a brother ready to spit. He had spent almost all morning doing this, spitting onto the kitchen roof below. Mama and Tato were at work or he'd never have dared. "Yuri, you are gross," I told him as I heard another *phtt* hit the kitchen roof.

"*Dyakuyu.*"

That means thank you. Trust Yuri to think being gross was a compliment.

I didn't say any more; we would only get into

an argument and I didn't have time. Instead, I inspected my boots. Mud was still caked to the soles after last week's training when it had rained and rained for the whole session and turned the field into a swamp. Still, at least the mud made them look bigger. My feet had grown so much that they pinched my heels and toes harder than Mrs Gres, my old schoolteacher, used to pinch naughty pupils' cheeks.

"If you like, you could use that spit to clean these for me," I told Yuri.

Yuri did not respond to my kind offer. Instead he carried on hoiking.

I spun round. "You still have chores to do, you know," I reminded him.

"Such as?"

"Such as looking after Sofi." Sofi is our three-year-old sister.

"She doesn't need me," Yuri replied, levering himself away from the window and going to sit on her camp-bed, wedged across from ours. "She's watching *SpongeBob SquarePants* with Uncle."

I shoved my boots into a carrier bag. "Wash the breakfast things, then."

"I *daren't*. I might have a heart attack with the excitement."

"Funny boy!" I mumbled and dashed downstairs.

In the hallway, the door to the front room was slightly ajar. I did not wish to disturb vital TV-viewing, so I hastened through to the kitchen and out into the back garden.

Uncle's back garden was long and narrow with a cracked cement path down the middle. To the left of the path was an overgrown vegetable patch and to the right was what had once been a rose garden. Casting long shadows over both sides were brick walls straddled with thick ivy and honeysuckle. I loved it. We'd never had a garden in Lviv.

I sat on the back step, scraping the hard mud off my boots and feeling quite content – until I felt a plop on my head and looked up to see Yuri grinning down at me. My hair! He had spat on my hair!

I jumped up, outraged, and called him names
I would never have dared to use if Mama or Tato
had been home.

"Hey, hey, hey!" a voice behind me chided.
I turned to see Uncle looking at me. "That is no
way to talk to your brother."

"He spat on my head!" I explained, blushing.

Uncle chuckled. "If a bird poops on your head
they say it is good luck."

"Yuri's not a bird! He's a *ropukha*..."

"A what?"

"A toad. A dirty toad."

"Ah! Of course. I forget words these days. I forget
them in English and I forget them in Ukrainian. What
can you do, eh? What can you do when your brain
turns to mush?"

"Don't feel bad. It's a long time since you lived
there," I told him. He left Ukraine in 1947. Babka
– my grandma and his sister – hasn't seen him since
then. I glanced up at the bedroom window. If only

I could say the same about my brother!

Uncle shuffled forward, his gnarled hands curled round the handle of his walking-frame as if glued to it.

"Do you need help to the lavatory, Uncle?" I asked, for that was the main reason he ventured into the garden.

The lavatory was at the very end in a tiny brick building. There was one upstairs, of course, but untll he had his hip operation Uncle couldn't manage the stairs, so Tato had fixed up the old outdoor one for him. I was glad I didn't have to use it; the place was cold and damp – but Uncle didn't seem to mind.

"No, no. I'm fine as long as I take it steady," he replied.

Quickly, I kicked away my boots so he would not trip over them and stood aside so he could pass. I glanced behind us, into the house. "Is Sofi all right, do you know?"

"Sofiya is fast asleep, like an angel."

"I'll walk with you, then."

It was much harder walking slowly than quickly. The only thing to do was talk a lot.

"I'm going on the football trip this afternoon," I told him.

He glanced at me and smiled, his bushy dark eyebrows overlapping each other like a swan's wings. "Ah yes. The World Cup."

"Yes."

"I remember when England won the World Cup in 1966."

"Do you?"

"I watched it on TV in someone's house – someone I worked with in the hosiery factory. I didn't have a TV then. Not many did."

"No?" I asked, keen for him to tell me more. Unlike Yuri, who always pulled a bored face when Uncle began to reminisce, I enjoyed listening to his stories – especially when they were about football.

"And when Hurst scored that fourth goal! Oh! Everyone went crazy."

"I bet."

"Someone knocked over the standard lamp. It crashed to the floor and landed on my shoes, breaking the light bulb. There were splinters of glass in my socks."

"Ouch."

"I didn't mind. I was happy too. I was always happy for anyone to beat the Germans..." He paused, a thoughtful look on his face. "What I didn't agree with was the England team being called heroes afterwards. It was an achievement, yes. But heroes? No, no, no."

I grinned up at him, knowing what he meant. "Not compared with Kolya and the others, eh, Uncle?"

"Exactly." He nodded, his dark eyes suddenly alight. "Exactly."

Of all the stories Uncle had told me from his childhood, this was my favourite: about when he had watched a team called FC Start take on the German team Flakelf during the Second World War. The things he had told me about that match had made my hair stand on end. Every time I think of

Uncle actually being there, I am filled with awe.

I was about to ask him a question when he stopped and began fumbling in his cardigan pocket for his hanky. I waited as he wiped his mouth, returned the hanky and looked round with a frown on his face, as if he had forgotten what he was doing outside.

"Keep going, Uncle, you're nearly there," I urged.

"Nearly there? Hah! A snail would be quicker," he replied with a shake of his head. "Tell me about your World Cup, Veronika."

"Mine? Oh, OK. Well, we'll play lots of matches because the Under 11s is the most popular age range."

"That's good. You will be fit for the new season, then."

"And we're staying in something called a chalet. It's like a little wooden house."

"You must be very excited."

"I am – although we have to share rooms. I hope I get to share with someone I like."

"Whoever you get can't be worse than Yuri, huh?"

"True," I agreed, even though it wasn't, quite. There was one person on the team that Yuri would be heaps preferable to, and that was Jenny-Jane Bayliss.

For some reason she did not like me. She hadn't said anything as such; it was just a feeling I'd had, especially over the last few weeks. For example, on Tuesday at the training session to prepare for the tournament, Hannah asked us to get into pairs and Jenny-Jane walked off in the opposite direction, even though I was standing right next to her. Talk about making things obvious! I didn't know what I had done to Jenny-Jane but sharing a room with her for three nights would be *maytki*.

We reached the cherry-coloured doorway of the lavatory. "You have arrived!" I told Uncle, trying to sound cheerful.

He laughed. "What? So soon!"

2

Waiting for us on our return was Sofi, her wispy hair stuck to her chubby cheeks, her bottom lip jutting out. "You didn't come when I called you! You didn't come and I didn't know where you were."

"I was here, silly," I said, offering her my hand.

She yawned and slid her hand in mine. It was warm and sticky. "You didn't come," she repeated.

"Veronika, your boots," Uncle reminded me as I helped him and Sofi up the step.

"Yes, Uncle, thank you."

"Always look after your boots. Look after your boots and they will look after you…"

Before I could reply, a loud banging on the front door startled all three of us. They were here!

☆ ☆ ☆

Megan, my captain, beamed at me, her face shiny and excited. "Last port of call for Sherburn Sands! All aboard who's coming aboard!"

Behind her, I could see our minibus parked in the middle of the street. Several faces peered through the windows and my team-mates waved at me.

"Please wait," I said, panicking. "I just have to…" I turned, almost bumping into Yuri.

He dumped my bag at my feet. "Your belongings, ma'am."

I frowned at him. What was this? My brother being helpful! "Is everything in there? My toothbrush? My kit?" I asked anxiously.

He bowed. "Your toothbrush. Your kit. Your Highness."

"You're sure?" I said. If he was playing one of his tricks…

"I'm sure." He gave me a sheepish grin. "And about the hair thing?"

I had forgotten the hair thing! My scalp suddenly tingled. "Yes?"

"Just water."

"I believe you," I said, giving him a swift kiss on the cheek. I dashed into the front room and kissed Uncle and Sofi, too, then darted back into the hallway. "Be good," I instructed Yuri, hoisting my bag onto my shoulders and following Megan into the street. My heart began beating fast. It was actually happening. World Cup tournament, here I come! I turned and waved at the three figures at the window – and for a moment I didn't want to go. But only for a moment.

3

I was the last one to be picked up so the minibus was already full. As well as Megan, Lucy, Petra, Gemma, Eve and Jenny-Jane, there were Megan's mum and dad plus Hannah and Katie, the team coaches. Luckily, Lucy had saved me a seat near the back. Everyone high-fived me as I passed, apart from Jenny-Jane, who had her face turned to the window. See, I told you what she was like. I tried not to mind. It's a free world, right? Instead I snuggled up between Lucy and Eve and let my adventure begin.

By the time the minibus reached Sherburn Sands, two hours later, we had discussed many things, from how to tell if a hamster is dead or just asleep to what we thought our new teachers in September would be like. Most importantly, we had decided who would share rooms with whom during the tournament. Megan, Petra and Jenny-Jane would be in one chalet with Mr and Mrs Fawcett, and the rest of us would be in the other one with Katie and Hannah. I had squeezed Lucy hard, I was so relieved.

Only when Katie slowed down over the speed bumps did we stop talking, and then only for about a second.

"It's massive!" Petra gasped as we took in the lawns and blocks of buildings spreading out in front of us.

"There's the sea!" Lucy said, pointing at a gap between a glass-domed building and a huge marquee.

I craned my neck to look. The first time I had seen the sea was when we had flown over the English Channel to come to England. "It's wonderful," I whispered as the sun twinkled on the greeny-grey surface.

"It's just the sea." Jenny-Jane sniffed. "What's the big deal?"

☆ ☆ ☆

Katie pulled up in the car park in front of the accommodation block. There were several other coaches, cars and minibuses already there, and people were toing and froing with bags and boxes.

"Hang on while I find out what's what," Hannah told us, jumping down from the front seat. We watched as she approached a man in navy tracksuit bottoms and a green short-sleeved T-shirt. He nodded and ticked something off the list he was carrying.

Hannah bounded back to us. "Chalets seventeen and eighteen. Let's go, gang!"

Our chalets were so neat: freshly coated in white paint with their own lawn and flower-bed outside. Megan's group's chalet was directly above ours. Theirs had a veranda!

Inside it was bright and airy, with orange sofas and stripy beanbags and laminate wood flooring in one half of the living area, and an open-plan kitchen at the other. The bedroom that I was sharing with Lucy was so uncluttered compared with the one at Uncle's.

"I thought it would be bigger," Lucy stated, glancing round at the twin beds and beech dressing table between.

"I love it!"

"You love everything, Kozak!"

Hannah stuck her head round the door and grinned. "You two up for some grub?"

"Grub?" I asked in dismay. "Like a caterpillar?"

"Grub. Like a pizza!" She laughed.

I don't think I will ever learn all the slang words English people use.

4

The self-service restaurant was a short walk away. Inside it was teeming. I had never seen so many girls all at once! Girls of all ages, colours, shapes and sizes, and all making so much noise. It was a little overwhelming, but my stomach leapt with excitement. I had to pinch myself to make sure this was really happening.

After our meal of spaghetti bolognese and salad we headed to the marquee. Megan told me that this was where the presentations would be made on Sunday evening to the winners of this year's World Cup. "I've already planned the acceptance speech." She grinned.

We stuck together, finding a row of seats near the middle. As more and more teams entered, the noise in the marquee was crazy-loud until a group of adults arrived on the stage and everything calmed down.

There were about twenty of them. The man who had told Hannah where our chalet was now stepped up to the microphone. He said he was called Tom. He welcomed us and said how great it was to see so many faces, old and new. "It is a record turn-out." He smiled. "That just shows how girls' football is becoming more and more popular."

That made everyone cheer.

"Now for the exciting bit!" Tom announced. "Sally, the balls, please!"

From the side of the stage, a lady in a tracksuit pushed what looked like an enormous goldfish bowl on wheels in front of her. The bowl was full of ping-pong balls.

"What is this?" I asked Lucy.

"I think this is where we find out who we are during the tournament. When our team is called, they'll match it to a country."

"Oh."

"Fingers crossed we get England!"

"Oh yes," I said. "I see." I crossed my fingers like she and all the others on my row were doing.

We had quite a long wait. All the Under 9s and 10s had to go first. Then it was our turn. The first team to be drawn were called the Lincoln Griffins Lionesses. Tom sifted through the ping-pong balls and pulled one out from the bottom. "Brazil!" he announced.

"Yay!" voices from near the front cheered.

"Ooh," Megan whispered, "not bad. Brazil were my second choice, with the USA third."

Sally then read out the next team name: "Camelford Youth ..."

"... are Korea DPR!"

"Strong team," Lucy muttered.

One by one the Under 11s teams were matched to a country. Sweden, Denmark, Germany, Republic of Ireland, the Netherlands, Canada, Italy ... were all allotted but England, among others, still remained and so did we, among others. Then Sally read out our name: "The Parrs ..."

Lucy clung to my arm. We held our breath as Tom fumbled among the remaining balls.

"... are Ukraine," he announced.

I forgot I should have been waiting for England. "Wahoo!" I cried, and I jumped up and punched the air.

As soon as I sat back down I realized from the silent, grumpy faces that I had made a mistake. How many times had Mama and Tato told us that we must show respect for the country we now lived in? Jumping up and punching the air was not showing respect.

"I am sorry for yelling out loud," I said to everyone as we headed back to our chalets. "I got excited when the man said Ukraine."

"Don't worry about it," Katie said, patting me on the head. "I'd have done the same; it's only natural. What a coincidence, eh?"

"Yes," I said, "a big coincidence."

Behind me, Megan sighed. "I suppose us getting England was a long shot."

"It made it worse when it took ages for England to be drawn. We built our hopes up," Petra added.

"It would have been great, though, wouldn't it? I'd have loved to tell my brothers that I'd played for England. It's more than they ever will." Eve laughed.

I began to chew my lip. How disappointed they all were! Then Jenny-Jane piped up. "At least Nika's happy," she said, with a cold edge to her voice. "She's got what *she* wanted."

My heart raced. "I did not expect this…" I began apologetically, leaning forward so that I could look her in the eye.

"You got it, though, didn't you?" she snapped back.

Hannah, walking alongside Jenny-Jane, gave her a friendly hug. "Hey! There's no need for that! Just remember, the country you get doesn't really matter. The teams are still really only from Huddersfield or Plymouth or wherever."

"*Ukraine,* though! I'd rather have had Scotland than them." Jenny-Jane sniffed. "I mean, what have they ever won?"

"Ooh, I wouldn't go dissing Scotland, JJ. Dylan and Daisy will set their granny on you," Eve joked.

"Wales, then," Jenny-Jane muttered. "I'd rather have had Wales than lame Ukraine."

I lowered my head so no one would see my red face.

Hannah quickly clapped her hands together. "Right. Who's up for a game of charades back at ours?"

"Me, me, me!" Megan's dad said, jumping up and down.

Megan rolled her eyes at her mum. "Mum! You promised if I let you come he'd behave!"

Everyone laughed, me included. It was a relief to be able to focus on someone else.

5

The next morning we had to travel in the minibus to the playing fields. The Under 11s league was to be held at a secondary school, eight kilometres away. Both today and tomorrow we would be playing five matches. This sounds ridiculous, but each match is only six minutes each way, with breaks in between.

Tom and another of the organizers, Tamsyn, met us on the fields to tell us our schedule. "First to arrive! Well done! Ukraine, isn't it?"

"It is," Hannah replied.

At the mention of the word Ukraine, I felt my stomach clench. So far this morning, nobody had talked about *not* being England, but they hadn't talked about *being* Ukraine, either. I got the feeling everyone was "making do" with it.

I listened self-consciously as Tom told us the arrangements. "This morning, Ukraine, you're meeting Russia first, followed by Australia, then Sweden. This afternoon you take on China and the USA. Don't worry if you don't remember; there's a list on the board outside the changing rooms. Results will be recorded there – but just so you know, we've decided not to display goal difference this year."

"Why not?" Megan asked.

"In case any teams lose by several goals. We don't want to knock anyone's confidence." When he saw Megan's outraged expression he laughed. "I know, I know. Not my decision."

"I hate it when they treat us like babies," she complained.

Tom nodded, then continued, "Toilets and so on are in the changing rooms. Good luck."

We were already changed, so we didn't need to use the changing rooms. Instead, we inspected the empty group table, to see which other teams we'd be meeting. It looked like this:

Sherburn Sands 7th Festival of Football Fun
World Cup Competition
Girls' Under 11s Group 1

Team	P	W	D	L	Pts
Australia					
Brazil					
China					
Denmark					
Republic of Ireland					
Italy					
Korea DPR					
Russia					
Sweden					
Ukraine					
USA					

My heart sank when I saw that Ukraine were bottom but one. I knew the list was in alphabetical order, but it seemed like an omen. I could almost read Jenny-Jane's thoughts: "See, told you they were lame."

As I sat on the grass and pulled on my boots, a heavy feeling settled inside me. Was it only yesterday I'd perched so happily on Uncle's back step to clean them? I sighed, remembering how excited I'd been. How anxious to get going.

The boots began to rub as soon as I squeezed my feet into them. No matter, I thought, jumping up and beginning my stretches; no matter.

"Right, girls," Hannah said, gathering us round after our warm-up. "These matches are only short, but don't go tearing round the pitch. We haven't got any subs, so pace yourselves. I don't want you flaking out by lunchtime."

"OK," we replied.

"Now, let's have Megan in goal, with Petra and Lucy at the back for starters… Gemma, I'll have you central midfield, with Nika and Jenny-Jane assisting. Eve, you go up front. OK?"

"I'm on it, chief!" Eve said with a salute.

Hannah laughed and saluted back. "Let's go and enjoy ourselves. Remember, this is a fun tournament – right?"

Fun? It didn't feel much like fun at the moment.

6

I confess I did not play well in the games against Russia, Australia or Sweden.

I could feel my boots rubbing against my heels, sending shooting pains up the backs of my calves, with every step I took. It was agony, making me slow and clumsy. But if I was bad, it was nothing compared with Jenny-Jane.

I should make it clear that despite Jenny-Jane not being very nice to me sometimes, I still rate her as a player. She is like a mosquito, buzzing in and out, barging the opposition off the ball, holding possession for as long as she can – often longer than she should – before passing or shooting. She is brave and she is loyal.

Today, though, she was not any of these things. Today, whenever there was a fifty-fifty ball in her area, she seemed happy to let the opposition have it. There was no chasing. No tackling. No shouting. No bravery. This was not just for the first match, but for all of them. The mosquito had turned into a potato.

I suppose because our results were mixed – we lost to Russia one–nil, drew two-all with Australia and beat Sweden three–nil – nobody else noticed.

"Four points. Could be worse," Megan said simply as we gathered round the board at the end of the morning.

So that was that.

But if nobody else noticed Jenny-Jane's attitude on the pitch before lunch, they did after it. She hardly moved during the match against China. Potato? A statue of a potato, more like! Once, just as she was about to reach a loose ball she stopped dead, allowing the China defender, who'd been miles away, to pounce. The defender stared at her in disbelief, unable to believe her luck. We lost that one three–two.

☆ ☆ ☆

During the short break before our final match of the day, against the USA, Hannah took Jenny-Jane to one side. Everyone tried not to stare, and huddled round the bags and drinks.

"What's with JJ?" Gemma asked in a loud whisper. "I passed her the ball at least three times and she just ignored it."

"Same here," Eve said.

I glanced across to where Jenny-Jane was deep in conversation with Hannah. "I … I know what it is," I said quietly.

Everyone looked at me expectantly. "What?" Eve asked.

I hesitated, torn between not wanting to talk about Jenny-Jane behind her back and the need to explain. "I think it's because we are Ukraine and she doesn't want to be Ukraine."

Lucy frowned. "What? That's bonkers."

"She did take not getting England quite hard," Megan mumbled.

Petra snorted. "You can say that again. She kept going on and on all night. I told her to put a sock in it in the end, and Megan threw her pillow at her."

"Seriously?" Eve asked. "But Hannah explained about…" She cut her sentence short as Jenny-Jane stormed past us, her dark eyes flashing like a cornered cat's. We fell into an uneasy silence and looked everywhere but in her direction.

Just for the record, we lost to the USA, too. Three–nil. We needn't have lost, in my opinion; I thought the USA goals were avoidable, the first went in off Lucy's knee, the second and third after Megan fumbled catches she would normally have dealt with easily. That's the thing with seven-a-side football. One person's mood can affect everybody else's.

We were all quiet on the minibus afterwards. Mr and Mrs Fawcett tried really hard to get some sort of conversation going, but it didn't work and even they lapsed into silence. It was awful. How I wished

Tom had picked another country for us. Any country apart from mine.

When we arrived back in Sherburn Sands, Hannah jumped down from the driver's seat on one side of the minibus and Katie on the other. We all stood in the car park, waiting.

"OK, ladies and gentleman. It's free time now, but I think we could all do with a bit of a rest before we start any other group activities," Hannah said, sounding a little too bright, and she was careful not to look at any of us in particular. Instead she checked her mobile. "It's just coming up to quarter-past three. Let's meet again at half-four and go for a paddle in the sea before dinner. Last one in the water buys the ice-creams – deal?"

That idea seemed to cheer people up. "Deal," we chorused.

7

Once inside our chalet, Hannah went for a shower and the rest of us changed in our bedrooms. "I hope JJ sorts herself out," Lucy said as she pulled her Parrs shirt over her head. "I hate bad atmospheres."

"Mmm," I replied, trying not to wince as I undid my laces.

"I mean, I know it's a shame we're not England, but come on. Get over it."

I shrugged. I didn't really want to talk about it at all; it churned me up too much. Instead I told her how nice it would be to paddle in the sea.

"Nice and freezing cold." Lucy grunted, then foraged in her rucksack and pulled out a Manchester United T-shirt and matching shorts. On her feet she wore a pair of flip-flops.

"That's me done!" she declared.

I chose shorts, too, and a plain T-shirt, but I decided to keep my football socks on. My heels were still throbbing and I didn't dare take the socks off in case my skin peeled away – and it really, really felt as if it might.

Back in the living area, Eve and Gemma were watching TV, with Katie near by reading *Heat* magazine. "Who's going to make me a cup of tea, then?" Katie asked.

"I will!" I volunteered, glad of an activity to do.

"Thanks, chuck. Black, two sugars."

"Really? That is how my uncle likes his." I glanced at the telephone on the worktop. A sudden urge to talk to my family overcame me. "Katie ... would it be OK to call home?"

She looked at me searchingly for a moment. "Sure," she said.

"I won't be long ... just a few minutes."

"Go for it."

I dialled as I waited for the kettle to boil. The

phone rang and rang. Where was everybody? I knew Mama and Tato would be at work, but Yuri should have been there. Or Sofi, even. My eyes prickled. "Answer, answer," I willed, desperate to hear a familiar voice before I faced Jenny-Jane again.

Finally, Uncle answered. "Yes? Who is it?"

I smiled. He did not have the best telephone manner. "Uncle. It's Nika."

"Veronika! How are you?"

"Good," I said.

"I am glad you called. It is so quiet here. Yuri and Sofi have gone with your mother to the library."

"Is Mama not at work?"

"Not today, no."

There was a long pause. I had nothing to say and yet so much to say – but it was difficult in a room full of people.

It was Uncle who broke the silence. "So, how is the tournament going? How many goals have you scored? Ten? Twenty?"

"None!"

"None! Oh dear."

"I…" My throat felt jammed with words. I glanced across at everyone. Nobody seemed to be listening, but… I took a deep breath and changed to Ukrainian. "Actually, it's not going so good, Uncle."

He continued to speak in English. "Oh? How come? It is badly organized?"

"No. It is well organized. It's just that we were all given a country for the World Cup, and everybody wanted to be England but we got—"

"Don't tell me. Scotland!" Uncle interrupted.

"No. Ukraine."

"Ukraine? Oh-ho! That is fantastic."

"Not really," I said and told him what had happened. "One of the girls isn't happy. She isn't even trying to play."

"She is a poor sport?"

"I guess. I think she just thinks it is a rubbish team because we haven't won anything."

"Haven't won anything? Puhh! That's all she knows."

"Well, we haven't won the World Cup, have we. Or the European Cup, either."

"So what? Sometimes there are things more important in sport than cups and medals. Sometimes there is honour at stake. And pride. And even life." His voice rose higher and higher, as it did when he became emotional.

"I know, but…"

"Veronika!" Uncle said sharply. "Do you remember the story I told you about FC Start?"

"Of course, Uncle. It is my favourite."

"Well, I only told you half of it."

"Half?"

"Yes. I have only told you up to the end of the match. I have never told you what happened afterwards, have I?"

"Afterwards? What do you mean? What happened afterwards?"

"Afterwards was when I fully understood the true meaning of bravery in sport." He hesitated then. "It is a little harrowing, though. Maybe you are too young."

"Tell me, Uncle. I need to know."

He took a deep breath. "Yes," he said. "I think you do."

So he told me. He told me and I listened. I listened and I listened. I listened with tears running down my cheeks that I had to wipe away quickly, hoping no one would notice. I listened with such a pain in my heart I thought I must have angina like Babka gets sometimes.

"So, Veronika Kozak," Uncle said finally. "When the time is right, you tell her to stick that in her pipe and smoke it."

It was a confusing instruction. "I don't think she smokes, Uncle."

"Just tell her!" he rasped.

"I will."

"Promise?"

"Promise."

8

I turned to see everyone looking at me.

"Oh," I said. "Er … hello."

"Hello." Katie grinned, sliding past to rinse out a beaker in the sink.

My hand flew to my mouth. "Oh, your tea! I'm sorry! I forgot."

"I forgive you; thousands wouldn't."

Lucy came to stand next to me. "You're really pale. Are you OK?" she asked.

I gave her a tight smile. "Yes, I am fine," I lied. In fact, I felt a little woozy, like you do when you have come out of a dark cinema and it is still light.

"You were talking really fast in Ukrainian," Gemma said. "Not that we understood any of it."

Eve wriggled her eyebrows. "Or that we were eavesdropping or anything."

"I'm fine, really. It was something my uncle was telling me. I just need a minute to myself..."

Eve promptly told me I couldn't have one. "It's twenty to five and no way am I buying the ice-creams."

I glanced at the clock in disbelief. Had I been on the phone that long? Dazed, I began to follow Eve and Gemma – but Lucy tugged my arm.

"It's OK, I'm fine," I reassured her again, thinking she was still worried about me.

"I know. I heard you. I just thought you might like to put some shoes on first."

I laughed. "Oh yes ... shoes... Good idea!"

The beach was busy. There were lots of girls there, presumably from the tournament, and several families were camped out on blankets surrounded by buckets and spades and cool boxes.

"The tide's coming in," Lucy said. "I wish I'd worn my cozzy on now. Come on – race you to the sea."

"In my trainers?" I asked.

"Take them off if you like," she said. "Barefoot's

best on sand." She pelted towards the sea, where everyone else was already larking around.

I slipped off my trainers but left my socks on, and followed more cautiously. I had never walked on sand before. It was all new to me.

I liked it. I liked the warm softness of it and the way it moulded round my feet as I walked, but then the dry sand turned to wet, muddy silt and I had to stop. I couldn't go any further without dirtying my socks and I didn't want to do that.

I sat down on a patch of warm sand and gingerly pulled off first one, then the other. The skin on my heel stuck but it didn't peel away. Instead, it bulged as soon as it was released, with one huge blister about the size of an apricot on my left heel and two smaller but equally tender ones on the right. I stared at them in fascination for a second before leaping up and running to catch my friends.

Everyone had left their shoes and flip-flops in a pile by an abandoned sandcastle, and they were all either standing at the edge of the water letting it wash over their feet or, like Eve and Gemma, jumping and splashing around further in. For a moment I forgot my problems with Jenny-Jane. I forgot my blisters as the stinging cold seawater numbed all feeling in them. I almost forgot the conversation with my uncle. The sea. The sea was incredible! Ukraine only has seas to the south and both were over six hundred kilometres from Lviv. To have a resort like Sherburn Sands only two hours from home... What a gift. I stared into the distance as the water caressed my feet, lost in thought.

"Enjoying yourself, Nika?" Mrs Fawcett asked. She was standing close by, her jeans rolled up to her knees.

I shivered. "Yes," I said, fixing a smile on my face, "very much."

"Good." She then began telling me about the hours she used to spend with her sister, Mandy, climbing from one rock pool to another, searching for periwinkles and sea lemons and anemones and other interesting-sounding specimens.

I could not say "anemone" at all. "Anenemy?"
I repeated. "Amenimy?"

Mrs Fawcett began to spell it for me – but we were interrupted by an ear-piercing shriek. Eve, a few metres further into the sea than we were, had been drenched from head to foot. "That wave was bigger than I expected!" she said, giggling, coughing and spitting out seawater all at the same time. Gemma and Lucy were doubled up with laughter – but then another wave washed over, drenching them too.

Everyone was laughing now. Megan and Petra, not wanting to be left out, ran straight in, followed by Hannah and Katie. Only Jenny-Jane held back, her face obscured by the breeze whipping at her long hair, her hands dug deep in her trouser pockets.

"Go on, Nika," Mrs Fawcett said, giving me a nudge. "In for a penny, in for a pound."

Yes, I thought. Why not? Time to lighten up, Nika! I splashed through the water and began leaping over the oncoming waves. Sometimes I managed to clear them and sometimes I didn't. One thing was for sure: within seconds I was as wet and happy and noisy as everyone else – until the moment I took a long step back to scissor-jump over a really high wave and the back of my left foot rammed into something sharp. If Eve's shriek had been piercing I don't know what mine was. My heel hurt so much I almost fainted. I immediately began to hop to the dry sand, with everyone following me.

"Are you all right, Nika?"

"What happened?"

"Look! Her foot's bleeding loads."

"It's a good thing Mum's here. I knew it was useful bringing a nurse along," Megan said.

Mrs Fawcett took one look at my foot and said we'd need to get back to the chalet quickly to clean it. Before I knew what was happening, Hannah and Katie had hoisted me into the air, their arms plaited under me like the seat of a swing. Now that I'd left the water, my foot was stinging so much all I could do was squeeze my eyes shut and pray.

Back in the chalet, I perched on one of the high stools at the breakfast bar. My foot was outstretched on another stool, as Mrs Fawcett cleaned my injury. I think she used up nearly everything in the first-aid box. "At least it was a rock and not glass or a rusty tin you hit, so you don't need a tetanus jab. Fortunately it just sliced through the blister and not bone," she said, screwing the lid back on the tube of antiseptic. There was a chorus of "yeuw" from the crowd. "We'll keep this dressing on for tonight and see how it is in the morning. If it looks inflamed, I'll get you straight to the hospital."

"Those blisters. No wonder you were limping!" Lucy said, her eyes full of concern.

"I'll be OK now. Really," I said, looking at her, then at everyone else. I felt my cheeks burn. I'd done it again: caused problems and ended up being the centre of attention. "I am sorry for spoiling the fun."

"Don't be," Petra said; "it's not like you did it on purpose."

"Accidents happen," Mrs Fawcett reassured me. "I'd be out of a job if they didn't!"

Most of the others gave me a sympathetic smile. Not Jenny-Jane, though. Of course not. "Huh," she said. "Well, we can kiss the tournament goodbye now, can't we?"

Everyone turned to look at her. "What do you mean?" Megan asked.

"We're a player short, aren't we? How're we supposed to play seven-a-side with only six of us?"

My heart began to pump fast. "I'll be fine tomorrow. I feel much better already with the bandage and everything," I told her coldly.

"Yeah, right," Jenny-Jane muttered. "Fat lot of use you'll be limping around. Who's that hobbling about on the touchline? Oh yeah, the lame Ukrainian."

That did it! Anger darted through me, sharper than any rock. I curled my hands into small, tight fists until the knuckles hurt. If Jenny-Jane wanted a fight, she could have one. I hobbled right up to her. "Take that back. Take that back now!"

"What?" she asked innocently, holding her hands in the air.

"About me being a lame Ukrainian."

"But you are a lame Ukrainian. You're lame and you're from Ukraine. I'm just stating facts. What's wrong with that?" She looked around her for back-up, but none came.

Even if it had, it wouldn't have mattered. I was blind and deaf to everything except this smelly *ropukha* in front of me. I poked my finger in her chest. "Don't lie! You don't mean lame because I can't walk, you mean lame because you think my country is useless." She opened her mouth to deny it but I saved her the trouble. I was not the polite, respectful immigrant girl now, letting her comments pass. "For your information, Ukraine is not useless.

It's brilliant and it's brave!" As I spoke my face got nearer and nearer to hers – but she didn't flinch.

"Brilliant?" she barked. "Huh! If it's so brilliant, why are you all coming over here, then? Why don't you stay there in your oh-so-brilliant country?"

"JJ!" Someone near by gasped. Hannah or Katie, perhaps. I didn't know or care.

"That's *my* business, you racist!" I yelled and grabbed a handful of her hair.

Immediately she grabbed my wrist and dug her nails into it. "Racist? Get stuffed! If I was a racist I wouldn't speak to Eve or Tabinda, would I?"

But I wasn't listening. Instead I tugged harder on her hair, with both hands now, and would have pulled every dirty strand out by the roots if someone hadn't pressed their fingers hard into my shoulders. I turned to see Katie behind me, her eyes wide with dismay, and my anger vanished in an instant. What was I doing? Fighting and screaming in front of the people I admired so much. My shoulders slumped and I began to tremble.

Katie released her grip slightly. "It's all right," she soothed; "it's all right."

"Um … I think it might be a good idea if we all went to our separate chalets for a while to cool off…" Hannah began, her hands on Jenny-Jane's shoulders. "We can meet at dinner, OK?"

"Suits me," Jenny-Jane muttered, her eyes boring into mine.

For a moment I thought it suited me, too, but as I turned to go, I stopped. Meeting again at dinner wouldn't change anything. Too much had been said. Unless Jenny-Jane and I sorted this out now, things would only get worse and worse until we exploded again. And the way I – *we* – felt I knew we would explode again. I did not want that. "Just a minute, please," I said quietly.

Katie looked at me closely, like a zookeeper deciding whether to release an agitated animal back into its pen or not. I gave her a pleading smile and she let go of my shoulders.

For the first time, I glanced round the room.

Everyone looked either shocked or embarrassed.

"I ... um ... could you all sit down? I want to tell you a story..." I said.

The shocked and embarrassed expressions turned to puzzled ones.

"About a football match..." I continued, perching on the stool again. I swallowed and waited.

No one seemed to know what to do.

"Look, I know you all wanted to be England in the tournament, and I am sorry we aren't. Truly, I am. And Jenny-Jane" – she shot me a dirty look and folded her arms across her chest defiantly – "you should be proud of your country for once winning the World Cup against West Germany..."

"Thanks for letting me know," she muttered.

"But England aren't the only team to have won a big match against them. Not just West Germany but *all* Germany."

"What? In a World Cup final?"

I tilted my chin. "No. It was much more important than that!"

"How could it be? What's more important than winning the World Cup?"

"Sit down and I will tell you. I will tell you something that will make you wish you came from such a brave and noble country as Ukraine."

Jenny-Jane strode over to the seating area and dragged one of the beanbags across the floor, placing it right in front of me. She sat on it, her arms folded, a haughty look on her face. "Go on, then," she challenged. "I'm all ears."

Her action seemed to break a spell. "Wait for me," Lucy declared and grabbed the other beanbag.

Megan and Petra joined in then. "Hang on! Hang on!" they cried, manoeuvring the sofa round.

The atmosphere changed a little. Instead of tension, there was expectation. Before I knew it, the whole team were sitting at my feet, with Hannah and Katie perched on the sofa arms and Mr and Mrs Fawcett leaning against the windowsill at the back.

Looking around, I was suddenly aware of the task I had set myself. I didn't know if I'd be able to tell it all properly. What should I leave in? Or rather, what should I leave out? The ending Uncle had divulged today was so grim.

"Come on, Kozak. Once upon a time..." Eve began for me.

Once upon a time. Of course! I would tell Uncle's tale like a story in a book rather than a true account. I would pretend my uncle was a character. Then maybe I wouldn't be quite so emotional when I thought of him and my poor babka during that time, experiencing those dreadful things. Instead of using their names, I chose the names of my favourite male and female football players: Andriy after Andriy Shevchenko and Darina after Darina Apanaschenko. Taking a deep breath, I began.

10

"Once upon a time there was a thirteen-year-old orphan called Andriy. He lived with his ten-year-old sister, Darina, in the glorious city of Kiev, the capital of Ukraine. One day, he—"

"Why were they orphans? What happened to their mum and dad?" Petra asked.

"They died during the Holodomor," I said, not having time to think up anything but the truth.

"The Holodo what?"

"Holodomor. It means death by starvation."

"What was it? Like a famine?" Lucy asked.

So much for me just sticking to the description of the match! But I realized that, like with all good stories, you had to build up the background first. I looked at my team-mate and told her what I knew from things Babka had told me. "No, it was not a famine. This was not a natural disaster. You see, Andriy and Darina were not from Kiev originally. They were born in the countryside many kilometres away. They were brought up on a collective – a small farm – and lived with their family there. But it was a bad time for them. Ukraine was part of Soviet Russia, and Stalin, the Russian leader, decided the Ukrainians were too independent and needed to be taught a lesson. He ordered that they weren't allowed to eat anything they grew, and all their crops were confiscated. If the farmers did try to keep any food they were punished."

"But everyone's got to eat!" Megan stated.

"Stalin obviously didn't think so. Millions died, including Andriy and Darina's parents. Luckily, a kind neighbour called Marina, who had lost her husband and daughters, took the children to live with her brother and his wife in Kiev."

"And were the brother and his wife really cruel to the children?" Petra asked.

I frowned, not understanding why she would think

this – then I realized she thought I was telling a fairy-tale. I wish! "No, no, they were kind. Ukrainians are very welcoming people. Andriy and Darina grew into fine, sturdy children and attended school and did other normal things…"

"Minty." Petra nodded.

"And, like lots of his school friends, Andriy's passion was football. He followed the city's best team, Dynamo Kiev…"

"I've heard of them!" Gemma cried.

"Me, too," Lucy added. "We played them in the Champions League."

"They were a very good team," I said, staring at Jenny-Jane, daring her to contradict me. "One of the finest in Eastern Europe at the time. Andriy's favourite player was Nikolai Trusevich, the goalkeeper, whom everyone called Kolya."

"Kolya?" Megan repeated.

"Kolya. Kolya was a gentle man off the pitch, but on the pitch he would thrill the crowds by taking such risks! He was strong and brave and fearless.

He also had his own style of doing things. Instead of catching the ball and then kicking it upfield, he often just kicked it. I know keepers do this nowadays, but back then it was unusual. The crowd thought it was amusing, but it meant he gave his side more chances to attack because the ball was further forward.

"Of course, there were other good players, too. The baby-faced defender Alexei Klimenko, who came from a famous circus family, and the nippy winger Makar Goncharenko..." I paused. I could see the Ukrainian names were difficult for my team-mates to take in, so I didn't go through the whole team. In truth, I could not remember all of them anyway.

"But it was Kolya whom Andriy adored above all," I continued. "He would try to sit behind the goal during the match, to be close to him, to watch his antics. Because of Kolya, Andriy decided that when he grew up he, too, would be a goalkeeper..."

"Like me." Megan beamed.

"Then the war started. Of course, with the war, all professional football was halted. The players joined the army. The leagues were suspended…"

"They were here, too," Mr Fawcett added. "I remember my dad telling me."

"Oh! I wish my dad were here!" Lucy piped up. "He loves history."

I nodded shyly. I seemed to have engaged everyone so far. Except one. Jenny-Jane was as stony-faced as when I had started. Never mind. I would not let her put me off. I cleared my throat and continued. "At the same time Andriy left school and got a job as an errand boy in Bakery Number Three…"

"I'd love to work in a bakery. All those cakes," said Eve, licking her lips.

I paused again. We'd never get to the end with all these interruptions! "It wasn't a little bakery, with buns and cakes in the windows like you have here on the high street," I explained. "It was a huge factory where the shifts were twelve hours long.

And you weren't allowed to eat any of the bread.
If you did you'd be dismissed instantly."

"Oh," Eve said. "I'd be sacked on day one, then."

"OK, so, with the war, things were tough – but
then things had always been tough. The Kievans
managed. People went to work. Life carried on.
Then Hitler decided it would be a good idea
to invade Russia so he pointed his troops at
Stalingrad. And guess which city was *en route*
to Stalingrad? Kiev!"

"Uh-oh," Petra murmured.

"The German army marched on our beautiful city.
For months the Russians and the citizens fought
bravely to save the capital, but eventually they
were defeated. Kiev – or what was left of it after
it had been bombed and set alight – was under
German occupation.

"Life was a nightmare. The Germans treated the
people worse than Stalin had. Andriy went to work
every day feeling terrified, wondering if he'd make it
back home alive or if he'd get a bullet in his head for

no reason other than that he was Ukrainian.

"Then, one day, he had the shock of his life –
but in a good way! He turned up for work, and who
should be sweeping out the bakery yard but Nikolai
Trusevich himself. The great Kolya! Only now he was
not so great. He limped as he swept and seemed to
have aged beyond his years. But still, the Dynamo
goalkeeper it was. It turned out that the manager of
the factory, a guy called Kordik, had given him a job.
Like Andriy, he was a big Dynamo fan and had taken
the player in."

"Cool. Did Andriy talk to Kolya? Did he get his
autograph?" Lucy asked.

"No; he was too shy. But he caught glimpses of
him whenever he could and once, when he passed
close to him, Kolya winked at him…"

"I'd have so asked for his autograph," Eve said
with a shake of her head.

"They probably didn't have autograph books in
those days," Petra told her.

"Oh yeah. I never thought of that."

"Ahem. Is it OK if I continue my story now?"

Eve grinned. "Yep. Carry on, Nika."

"Thank you. Where was I?"

"Kolya working at the bakery," Megan quickly informed me.

I nodded, grateful that she was listening so attentively. "Right. Kolya was working for Kordik. Now Kordik employed other sportsmen as well. Gymnasts, cyclists, boxers – in fact, people from every sport going, but it was footballers Kordik favoured most, and soon other players joined the workforce. Before long he had half the Dynamo Kiev team baking bread and cleaning the ovens! He hired players from other local teams too, such as Lokomotiv. Then something happened that excited Andriy beyond belief: Kordik persuaded the German authorities to let him get a team together. They called it FC Start and they played in red."

"Like us!" Eve pointed out.

"Like us." I smiled. "They trained at a disused ground on Kerosene Street, behind the bakery. After a while, they began playing proper matches. The authorities were happy to let this happen. They liked sport, too, remember, and the bakery team was put in a mini league with a mixture of factory and army teams. The difference was that FC Start were really good. Even though the players were unfit and injured and half-starved, they were still professional footballers. They were still skilled. That summer they beat every team they came across. Not just by one or two goals, either. In the five matches they played, they scored thirty-two goals and had only three goals against."

"Not bad!" Eve whistled.

"Word got round. More and more people came to watch the matches. At last the people had something to lift their spirits. Something to cheer about. Football! But the Germans didn't like it one bit, this rag-bag team outclassing everyone and becoming more and more popular. So they sent in their best team, Flakelf – the players were mainly pilots and aircraft crew – to put Start in their place.

And guess what? Start beat them five–one!"

"Get in!" Megan called out.

"At work the next day, Andriy overcame all his shyness and dashed up to the goalkeeper and flung his arms round him. When Kolya patted the top of his head in response, Andriy vowed never to wash his hair again…"

Everyone laughed, giving me a chance to shift my weight and change position. I stood up so I could face everyone. My heel didn't throb at all now, it was so well padded. I stooped nearer my attentive team-mates and dropped my voice. I was coming to the main part of the story and I wanted to give it a proper build-up.

"That should have been that. There were no more games to play. It was August – well beyond the end of the season. Then Flakelf's coach demanded a rematch. The Germans were supposed to be the Master Race, superior in everything, right? No way could these dirty Ukrainians be allowed to get away with such a fluke result.

"Posters advertising the 'revenge' match were put up throughout the city. It was set to take place three days later, on August the ninth, a Sunday. Andriy couldn't wait."

"That's this Sunday!" Lucy shouted out. "This Sunday is August the ninth."

"As in tomorrow," Petra added.

Goose bumps prickled my skin. How strange that the dates should be the same. It threw me for a moment and I forgot where I was.

"Andriy couldn't wait," Megan prompted.

I nodded. "That's right. Andriy couldn't wait. Neither, it appeared, could anybody else. That hot Sunday afternoon it seemed as if the whole of Kiev was heading for the ground. The men had a spring in their step and were talking animatedly about tactics and predictions as to who would score first. The women had dressed for the occasion, putting traditional strands of lace in their hair. The kids were noisy and boisterous, caught up in the jolly atmosphere.

"But the nearer to the ground the crowd got, the quieter they became. As they walked down Kerosene Street they became more and more subdued. Why? The whole street was lined with German soldiers, that's why. Armed German soldiers accompanied by their savage Alsatians.

"It was the same inside the ground, too: the whole of the grandstand, where some of the crowd had hoped to sit, was taken up by German officers and soldiers. The Start fans had to make do with standing on the opposite side, in the glaring sun.

"Andriy squeezed his way through to an area close to the back of one of the goals. Here he sat shoulder to shoulder with other children, on the edge of the running track that separated the pitch from the terracing. Every so often armed guards would walk by, their dogs panting and slobbering over any kids' shoes they happened to pass.

"All this made Andriy nervous, but as soon as the teams came onto the pitch, his heart soared at seeing FC Start standing so proudly in the middle of the field. Their strip might have been makeshift and second-hand, their boots borrowed and worn, but they were his team and he adored them.

"But a minute later his soaring heart almost stopped. When the Flakelf side gave the obligatory Nazi salute, Start did not. Instead they gave the forbidden Soviet greeting – *Fizcultura* – meaning long live sport. The crowd gasped but then burst into spontaneous applause. 'Ha!' Andriy heard a man behind him say. 'Up yours, Adolf!'

"The whistle blew. Start did not start very well! Flakelf were all over them…" I began to pace up and down restlessly. "Boy, did Flakelf cheat – but the referee ignored every nasty, deliberate foul, every dirty, shirt-tugging, elbow-digging, shin-scraping challenge they made. It was obvious whose side he was on! And it was Andriy's favourite who was getting the worst of it. Poor Kolya.

"The Flakelf forwards were on him every time he tried to make a save, kicking and shoving him hard. Undaunted, the determined keeper lunged for every ball that came to him. Then something dreadful happened. He dived at the feet of one of the forwards, stopping what would have been a certain goal – but the Flakelf forward, instead of checking himself, let his foot continue through the shot and kicked Kolya straight in the head. Andriy swore that the crunching sound would be heard all the way down Kerosene Street."

"Oh!" Megan gasped, putting her hand to her own head, as if feeling the blow.

"Kolya was knocked out cold! He lay in his goalmouth, unmoving. Andriy couldn't believe it! He was incensed. *'Porushenya!* Foul, referee! A dirty, dirty foul!' he called out as Kolya was carried off the pitch by his team-mates and Goncharenko took over in goal. 'Why are Flakelf being like this?' Andriy asked one of the men standing behind him. 'They weren't so dirty last time.'

"The man blew cigarette smoke into the air above the boy's head. 'Why? Look at all the Gestapo watching them in the grandstand.

Would you dare to lose in front of those swine?'

"But Andriy didn't care about that. He wanted only to know if his hero was still alive. Oh, the relief when Kolya struggled to his feet, helped by the trainer. Pale and shaky, the keeper limped to the touchline and indicated to Goncharenko that he was ready to go back in goal. The crowd whistled and clapped in admiration.

"The trouble was, Kolya wasn't anywhere near ready. Before long the Germans scored, silencing the home supporters. Flakelf went in even heavier with their tackles, but the more they fouled, the more angry the crowd became. Not just the Ukrainians, either, but the soldiers from other regiments in Kiev. Hungarians and Italians and Romanians. All football-loving nations, who had come to watch football, not this ... this mess.

"The bravery of the crowd in even daring to protest seemed to encourage Start. When a decision finally went their way – for a free kick – Kuzmenko blasted it directly into the net to equalize, giving the referee no choice but to award the goal. A few minutes later Goncharenko volleyed home the second. Start, realizing that the only way their goals would be allowed was by a direct shot, netted a third before half-time."

"Go Start!" Petra called out.

"You can imagine how ecstatic Andriy and the rest of the Kievans were. Going in three–one up at half-time against all odds. During the break Ukrainian songs rang round the ground and women waved their lace ribbons in unity. And guess what? There wasn't a thing the Germans could do about it.

"Well, in the second half Start played as if they had been living off roast chicken and caviar for weeks, not almost starving to death! Both sides scored twice more, but it was obvious Flakelf were never going to win. They knew it. The crowd knew it. The referee knew it. He even blew his whistle five minutes *before time* – FC Start, against all odds, had beaten that crack German side…"

"Yahoo!" Eve yelled, and everyone clapped.

"Wait," I said, holding up my hand. "This is not the end."

I gathered myself for the final part, the part that was still new and raw to me and the main reason that Uncle had called these men heroes. "What Andriy didn't know, and only found out later, was that at half-time, an SS officer had come to the Start changing room and warned them to lose the match ... or else."

"But they didn't – they played even better," Megan said, her eyes wide and anxious.

I held my head high. "Exactly. They ignored the warning. No way would they throw the match... They were too proud, too brave to do such a thing.

"A week later the Gestapo arrived at the bakery. They marched into Kordik's office, pushing him aside, and began to call out names over the tannoy. One by one, every single member of the Start team was arrested and marched away. One of them, Korotkikh, was shot the next day; the rest were sent to Siretz, a prison camp."

"Oh no," Lucy cried out.

I concentrated on the floor, my voice trembling. "The following February Kolya, Klimenko and Kuzmenko were shot too..." Someone gasped, but I didn't look up. I just continued, speaking quickly to get it over with. "Andriy heard it was meant to be random – that they just *happened* to be picked from a long line of prisoners in retaliation for something that had occurred outside the camp – but as the man who broke the news said, 'Strange that it just happened to be those three who were 'randomly' selected, huh?'"

"So they were shot just for playing football well? That's mad," said Eve heatedly.

"Just for being *Ukrainian* and playing football well," I said. "And everything was mad in those days."

"Is that it? Is that the end?" Megan asked, her voice almost a whisper.

"That's it."

"I wish you hadn't told us that last part," Petra said.

"It's too sad. I'd have preferred a happy ending, like that story from the First World War – you know, the one about how on Christmas Day the German and English soldiers stopped fighting and had a friendly football match."

"Sorry." I shrugged. "But that's what happened. I think Goncharenko and one or two others escaped, if that helps."

"Not really," Petra mumbled, wiping her eyes with the back of her hand.

I turned to Jenny-Jane. I had not looked at her since the beginning of my story. Surely she wouldn't mind being Ukraine in the tournament now? "I hope you can see what I meant about this match being more important than any World Cup," I said. I waited for her response.

"Maybe," she eventually replied.

I blinked. "Maybe?"

"Well, it doesn't make me want to do what you said."

"Excuse me?"

She shrugged her shoulders. "You said it would make me wish I'd come from your country. No way! It sounds well bad. People starving and being shot. Who wants to live somewhere like that?"

For a moment I simply stared at her in bewilderment, then I, too, shrugged my shoulders. What else could I do? I would never convince this girl of anything. There was a cabbage where her heart should be. I was tempted to walk off, intending never to speak to her again, but instead I held out my hand. Resentment was pointless with someone like this. "Come on," I said; "let's get some grub."

She looked up suspiciously, hesitated, then put her hand in mine. "All right," she mumbled.

11

Somehow we ended up walking to the restaurant together. At first, neither of us spoke. I did not mind. I had told my story. It was up to everyone who heard it to do what they wanted with it. I would keep my thoughts carefully folded away, close inside.

It was Jenny-Jane who broke the silence, and what she said surprised me so much that I stopped in my tracks.

"What?" I asked her.

"I said I'm sorry."

"You are? Why?"

"For sounding a bit ... um ... *uncaring* about your story. I wasn't dissing it. I thought it was interesting and that ... in fact, it's the best football story I've ever heard."

"Thank you."

"It just didn't make me want to be Ukrainian. I like being English. England's the best country in the world."

I sighed. She had missed the point. "I wasn't really asking you to be Ukrainian. I just wanted you to see that your country isn't the only one that ever won an important game."

"Maybe," she said and kicked a pebble into the gully between the path and the grass.

"But even if you can't see that, please, will you play properly tomorrow? For our team? Even though we are not England?"

"I always play properly." She scowled.

I couldn't let such a fib go. "No you don't. You didn't try at all today and you know it. You let your team down just because you don't like me."

She seemed genuinely astounded. "Eh?"

"You don't like me because I am foreign. And don't deny it because it's as plain as a pancake."

"I do like you," she mumbled.

"I don't think so."

"I do. You're all right … you don't whinge or faff about like some I could mention."

"Thank you … I think."

"But you've got to admit your lot always seem to get everything."

"My lot?"

"Foreigners. Immigrants. Asylum seekers. Whatever."

"What do you mean we get 'everything'?"

She glanced across at me. "Everything! Like you. You got the free place, for a start, and then you even got your own country in the draw…"

"The free place? To take part in the tournament?"

"Exactly. My dad said that was typical of foreigners, coming over here and getting everything for nothing. He says people like you are bleeding the country dry."

"How kind of him," I muttered. Tato and Mama were often being told this by people they worked with, too, even though they both did jobs nobody else seemed to want. It was most hurtful.

I took a deep breath. "Look, I did not ask for the free place. Hannah asked me to come. She said we were one player short and nobody else could go. I told her we did not have spare money for things like this, but she told me that was not a problem; there was a free place nobody else wanted."

"Oh."

"Did you want it?"

Jenny-Jane looked insulted. "Me? No way. We've got loads of money, we have."

That surprised me. Jenny-Jane never gave the appearance of having lots of money – not that it mattered to me whether she did or didn't. "So tell that to your father," I continued, trying to keep my voice level. "Tell him I never asked for anything. And tell him that both my parents work hard and pay taxes. We do not claim a penny from the state. Or steal your council houses."

"OK, keep your hair on. I was only saying."

But I did not want to keep my hair on. I wanted

her to know everything so she could tell her prejudiced family. "We only came to England to look after my uncle."

"Oh."

"My uncle – who, by the way, is the Andriy in the story I just told you."

My revelation made a bigger impact than I had expected. Jenny-Jane stopped dead. "What? The old boy in the window when we picked you up – he's Andriy?"

"Yes."

"For real?"

"For real."

Her mouth opened and closed again, then she shook her head as we resumed our walk. "That's amazing," she said finally.

I smiled. I couldn't have agreed more. My uncle was amazing and I was very, very proud of him.

"He's the reason we're here," I explained. "He is old now and he needs someone to look after him. When he wrote to my grandma asking if she knew of anyone who might want to come to England for a while, to help him, we agreed. Mama taught English at college, so she thought it would be good experience, and Tato agreed because he thought it would be an adventure. But the adventure isn't always an exciting one, I can tell you."

Jenny-Jane bowed her head. "No, I guess not."

"When Uncle passes away we shall probably return to Lvlv."

Jenny-Jane looked startled. "That's a shame."

"Is it? I thought you'd be happy with fewer foreigners around. You and your dad."

She cleared her throat noisily. "My dad does get things wrong sometimes."

"Uh-huh."

"And so do I."

My heart leapt then. I knew that such an admission was progress for someone like Jenny-Jane. "So you will play properly tomorrow? For our team?"

She scowled at me. "I told you already; I always play properly."

I scowled back. Why was she still denying it?

"Not today you didn't," I persisted.

She shoved her hands deep into her pockets.

"I couldn't," she mumbled.

"Couldn't?"

"I've got these stupid boots that are miles too big. Every time I try to run I slob out of them and nearly break my neck."

"Are you serious? Because of your boots? Not because we were Ukraine?"

"What are you? Deaf or something?"

"But why didn't you say anything?"

"I thought I could sort it out. After the first matches I stuffed some paper towels in the toes, but that just made it worse – they were too big *and* felt weird. Then when Hannah had a go at me before we played America..."

"You felt victimized?"

"Exactly! First we don't get England, then my boots start giving me grief, then the coach starts giving me grief. No wonder I got a cob on!"

I laughed then. I couldn't help it. I laughed so much.

"What's so funny? I bet you wouldn't like it. I bet you never get told off. Me? Every breath I take someone's on my back."

"I think," I said, sliding my arm through hers, "I have a solution to both our problems."

If the rest of the team were surprised to see me walking into the restaurant arm in arm with Jenny-Jane they didn't say anything. They were probably just relieved we hadn't killed each other.

Afterwards, we all went to the karaoke evening in the big marquee. It was so funny, especially when Petra and Megan went up on stage and sang *"I Predict a Riot"*.

"I predict a headache," Eve joked.

It was a good end to a strange day. That night I thought I'd dream about FC Start or Jenny-Jane or blisters – or all three – but actually, I just slept.

12

Next morning I woke feeling much happier.

Telling the story had been – what's it called? A
turning-point. Even my blisters had stopped hurting.
When she came to examine them after breakfast,
Mrs Fawcett said they were clean and healing well.
I should be fine to play.

"Thank you," I said. "You're very kind."

"And you're very brave." She smiled.

"It's just a few blisters. My boots were rubbing."

"Speaking of which," said Megan, dumping a
pair of black and white Puma VKs on the worktop.
"JJ's sent you these." They were top range. Maybe
Jenny-Jane's family were rich, after all.

I reached down for my carrier bag, feeling a little
embarrassed by my shabby specimens. "And these
are for her."

"Swapsies coming through," Megan said and disappeared with my boots under her arm.

When we arrived on the playing fields, everyone gathered round the fixture lists. The group tables had all been updated, so instead of being in alphabetical order, the teams were now ranked according to points. This is how it looked:

Sherburn Sands 7th Festival of Football Fun World Cup Competition
Girls' Under 11s Group 1 Round 6

Team	P	W	D	L	Pts
Brazil	6	5	1	0	16
Republic of Ireland	5	4	1	0	13
USA	6	4	1	1	13
China	5	3	1	1	10
Korea DPR	6	2	2	2	8
Denmark	5	2	0	3	6
Italy	5	1	2	2	5
Ukraine	5	1	1	3	4
Australia	6	0	4	2	4
Russia	6	1	1	4	4
Sweden	5	0	0	5	0

"Oh, what!" Megan spluttered when she saw that Ukraine were eighth equal out of eleven.

"Don't panic," Eve told her. "All we need is to win every game and for Brazil, the Republic of Ireland, China, Denmark, Italy and America to lose all theirs and we'll qualify. Pips."

Megan sighed. "Who've we got first?"

"That'd be Brazil."

"Brazil. As in the team who have dropped only two points? Oh well. I guess I'll save my acceptance speech until next year."

"No you won't," Jenny-Jane said, stepping forward and puffing out her chest. "We're Ukraine. We can overcome any odds."

Everyone looked at her in disbelief – apart from me. Since our talk, I knew she was on my side. And when Jenny-Jane's on your side, anything is possible. In that moment I believed her: we, the Ukraine Under 11s, could overcome any odds. For the first time in the tournament, I felt butterflies stir in my tummy. "You're right, JJ," I said. "We can."

"Well, if you two say we can, then we can!" Megan beamed. She threw her arm round my shoulder. "Nika, what's Ukrainian for football?"

"Er ... *futbol.*"

"Oh. Well, that's easy enough. And how about 'Here we go?'"

"*Idemo v pered.*"

"Eed-e-mo-view-per-ed?" Her pronunciation was terrible and my expression told her so. "Let's just stick with the eed-e-mo bit," she said. "OK, everybody. Let's hear it. Eed-e-mo, eed-e-mo, eed-e-mo..."

We "eed-e-mo"d all the way to the pitch.

"How're the boots?" I called out to Jenny-Jane as we took up our positions.

"They'll do."

"I'm sorry they're not as new as yours."

"I'm not fussed as long as they do the job."

"There's only one way to find out."

"Yep," she agreed, her eyes already sizing up the opposition. "There is."

I have been playing football since I was six years old, so I have played a lot of matches, but I have never felt like I did when I took up my position that day.

As I waited for the game to begin, my heart thudding in my chest, my stomach knotted with tension, I imagined this was how Kolya must have felt all those years ago. Of course, I knew that Ukraine v. Brazil Under 11s at Sherburn Sands could not compare in any way to FC Start v. Flakelf. And I knew that Brazil were really the Lincoln Griffins Lionesses and we were the Parrs, but the joy I experienced when I heard the referee ask, "Ready, Ukraine?" and the feeling of pride that burst through me when Gemma answered "Ready" was unlike anything I had felt before. The strangest thing was

I think the rest of my team felt it, too. Not just me, not just Jenny-Jane, everyone. They all seemed to be standing up straighter, taller, prouder, and Megan … Megan had her arm across her chest in the old *Fizcultura* salute, just like FC Start had. One by one, everyone copied her, and it took every ounce of strength I had not to cry.

Then the referee blew her whistle and I told myself to concentrate. I am glad I did! It was immediately obvious why Brazil topped the table. They moved the ball quickly, with almost every pass finding its intended player. Our goal area was soon under attack, and I played most of the first half supporting the defence. Luckily, Megan was alert, tipping one attempt over the crossbar and punching away two more at close range. Sadly, though, she couldn't stop a low shot from their sharp striker just before the half ended. The ball flew into the bottom left-hand corner to put them one up.

"Well played, girls! You've woken up today!" Hannah praised as we swapped ends.

"Just keep pegging away," Katie added. "Megan, let's see you getting some of those goal kicks further upfield so we can counter-attack faster."

A slow smile spread across Megan's face. "Kolya style," she said.

So Megan began taking her goal kicks "Kolya style". The first couple of times she over-kicked and sent the ball straight out, but about midway through the half she judged her kick beautifully, directing it straight down the middle. Gemma chested it down, while I ran forward into the box to join Eve. Gemma then lobbed the ball high into the air, where Eve rose to claim it – but her marker got there first. The defender headed the ball out, too high for me to do anything except watch. I thought it was going to dip over my shoulder so I kept my eyes on it, turning all the time until I had my back to the goal. Then as the ball started to drop, I stretched out my leg, leaned backwards and powered my foot through the ball.

Whoosh! The ball flashed over my head, straight

past the keeper and into the back of the net. An over-head kick! I had equalized with an overhead kick!

"Unbelievable!" Eve laughed as she helped me to my feet.

Jenny-Jane walked with me back to the centre spot. "Who do you think you are – Peter Crouch?"

"I don't know," I said, "but I couldn't have done it without your boots!"

The goal spurred us on, no doubt about it. It was Brazil's turn to defend hard, but though we pressed and pressed we just couldn't get the winner. When the referee blew for full time, the Brazil team applauded us. "Thanks. Best game yet," their striker told me as we gave three cheers.

Mr Fawcett also complimented us as we crossed to the next pitch. "That was one of the most exciting matches I've ever seen you girls play."

"You haven't seen anything yet," Megan said.

She was right. In our next four matches we fought for every ball. We found space. We passed and tackled and remembered what to do in set pieces. Best of all, we scored. We beat Korea three–one. We beat the Republic of Ireland four–three, with Jenny-Jane scoring the fourth from a direct free kick in the last minute. Gemma scored a hat-trick against Italy to which they had no reply, and in our final match I assisted both goals in our two–nil victory over Denmark.

When that final whistle went, we all gathered by the touchline in stunned silence. Then we stared at each other. "Am I dreaming or have we just won every match except the one against Brazil?" Megan asked.

"We've just won every match except the one against Brazil," Eve confirmed.

Megan nodded. "Thought so!" And she tipped the contents of her water bottle over her head.

Everyone thought this was a good idea and followed our captain's example.

"Oops!" Petra blinked, her face dripping purple. "I forgot I'd put Ribena in mine!"

14

We raced over to the pavilion area to check out the final table. Only the top two from each group would qualify.

There was a massive crowd round the board, so Lucy volunteered to elbow her way through.

"I will come too," I said, unable to stand the thought of waiting. We jostled our way as close to the front as possible. Lucy, being taller than me, saw the results first.

"Well," I said, "have we done it?" I knew there was a chance. After all, we had picked up thirteen points out of fifteen that afternoon and we'd lost only three matches altogether. Maybe, just maybe… "Lucy?"

She turned – and her disappointed face told me everything. "Missed it by three points," she said.

"What? Let me look."

She stood aside so I could see for myself. Even on tiptoes I could make out only the top half of the table because of the heads bobbing in front of me.

Sherburn Sands 7th Festival of Football Fun World Cup Competition

Girls' Under 11s Group 1 Round 11

Team	P	W	D	L	Pts
Brazil	10	7	3	0	24
USA	10	6	2	2	20
Republic of Ireland	10	5	4	1	19
Ukraine	10	5	2	3	17
China	10	5	1	4	16
Denmark	10	4	1	5	13
Australia	10	2	5	3	11

"Bum and bum and more bum," was Megan's response when she heard the news.

"Brazil and the others forgot to keep their side of the bargain and lose, then?" Eve asked.

Lucy nodded. "Sorry for letting you down, Nika."

"Letting me down?"

"By not getting Ukraine through to the final,"

Gemma said. "We were all trying for you. Especially as today's the anniversary of the revenge match."

"Nobody has let me down," I said. "We played like lions." I glanced towards Jenny-Jane. "Three lions."

"Seven lions, actually." Eve sniffed, rubbing her knuckles across her shirt as if polishing her claws.

"Who goes through from the other group?" Gemma asked me.

I shook my head. I hadn't even thought to check.

"Scotland and the Netherlands," Lucy told her.

"Scotland!" Jenny-Jane spluttered. *"Scotland!"*

"Yo! That's us, Jimmy. Bonnie Scotland," a chirpy voice behind us yelled.

We all turned to see a group of girls in purple tops and white shorts dancing in a wavy line. "Join in, then!" one of them called – and before she could protest, Jenny-Jane was seized round the waist by the girls at the end and made to dance with them.

"Help!" Jenny-Jane called out as she was whisked away, but we were too busy laughing.

☆ ☆ ☆

Later that afternoon we watched the finals. There was a buzz in the air, with all the teams who had been knocked out cheering on the ones who were left. Brazil met the Netherlands in the final and beat them three–one to take the Under 11s' cup. "At least we took a point off the winners," Megan declared.

In the evening we had the presentation. We were all given medals to commemorate the tournament; I tucked mine down the inside of my top so I could feel it close to my heart. I had meant it when I told everyone I didn't mind not going through to the finals. That didn't matter. What mattered were the memories I would have of Sherburn Sands. Jumping in the sea. Swapping boots with Jenny-Jane. Telling everyone about FC Start.

As we walked back to our chalets I glanced up at the night sky, wondering if maybe Kolya and the others had watched and listened to it all over the past few days. I hoped, if they had, they'd be happy to know that their story lived on.

15

The next morning we had to be out of the chalets by ten, so there was no time to do much apart from have breakfast and load up the minibus. While Lucy finished packing I took Jenny-Jane's boots back to her. She was in her bedroom, cramming the last of her clothes into her rucksack.

"Hello," I said. "I've come to return your Pumas." I thanked her for lending them to me and set them down reverently next to her toiletry bag.

Jenny-Jane glanced at them, then continued with her packing. "Nah – you keep 'em," she said, stuffing a pair of socks into one of the rucksack's side pockets.

"Oh, I couldn't!" I protested.

"Why not?"

"Because they're yours and they're nearly new."

"So?"

"Plus they are expensive."

She shrugged. "It makes no difference if they don't fit, does it?"

"They will fit one day, surely?"

"What, like when I'm ninety?" Jenny-Jane reached for her toiletry bag. "Go on, take them."

I felt uneasy. It was kind of JJ to offer me her new boots, but even if I took them I wasn't sure her mama would approve. I knew mine wouldn't. She would march me straight round to the house and say I had made a mistake. "Perhaps you could return them to the shop instead?" I suggested.

Jenny-Jane glanced sideways at me and scowled. "That's not a good idea."

"What do you mean? No receipt?"

Instead of an answer, her eyes flicked towards the open bedroom door. She walked across the room to close it. "Can I tell you something? Something secret?"

"Of course."

"Those boots fell off the back of a lorry."

"Did they? And yet they're not scuffed or damaged at all," I told her, picking one up to examine it.

Jenny-Jane frowned and then a smile spread across her face. I had never noticed before how Jenny-Jane's face changes when she smiles. It is like the sun coming out from behind clouds. "Yeah … bit of a miracle, really. But don't tell no one, will you? That's between me and you."

"Sure," I replied. Although I was a little unsure why it had to be a secret, I felt pleased Jenny-Jane had shared it with me. It showed how much closer we had become, and I couldn't wait for the new season to start.

"So you keep the boots, OK?" she said.

"If you are really, really sure…" I would work out what to tell Mama later.

"Course I'm sure. I wouldn't say so otherwise, would I?"

I knew that was definitely true. This was someone who always meant what she said. Smiling gratefully, I picked up the boots and cradled them in my arms, like I used to do with Sofi when she was a newborn. "Thank you," I whispered.

"And can I keep yours?" Jenny-Jane asked. "Because they're at the bottom of my backpack and I'll be well cheesed off if I have to undo everything."

I laughed. The rucksack looked like a fat and lumpy old tree trunk, sprouting things here, there and everywhere. "Oh, I wouldn't make you do that, not after all that careful packing."

"Cheers."

There was a tap on the door. "Time to go, people!" Megan called.

Jenny-Jane and I grinned at each other. Time to go indeed.

"Have you all enjoyed yourselves this weekend?" Hannah asked as we sat on the minibus, waiting for Katie to hand in the chalet keys.

"Yeah!' Megan replied, answering for all of us. "It's been wicked."

"It's gone too fast," Petra complained.

"I know. It always does," Hannah agreed.

Mr Fawcett sighed. "I'm so mad at myself for not bringing the camcorder."

"Then you could have caught our awesome comeback," Megan told him.

"And Petra's impression of a blackcurrant afterwards," Eve said. "That was classic."

"Not forgetting Nika's amazing overhead kick," said Lucy, digging her elbow into my ribs.

"There're women on the senior team who couldn't have pulled that off," Hannah said, grinning at me.

I hid my face in my hands. I am not very good at being praised. And my team-mates did not help by leaning over and mussing up my hair and squeezing me to pieces.

"Stand up and take a bow, sista-wiv-da-blista," Eve teased. Then they all began rocking from side to side, rapping out "Sista-wiv-da-blista" over and over again. Crazy.

I was so relieved when Katie arrived and we could get going. "Aw, poor Nika." She laughed when she saw my new scarecrow hairstyle. "We'd better drop you off first so you can recover."

"Thank you," I said, frantically trying to flatten my hair back into place.

Hannah started the engine. "What was that song you guys were singing yesterday? For 'Here we go'?" she asked.

"Eed-e-mo," everyone chorused.

"Let's hear it, then."

"Eed-e-mo … eed-e-mo … eed-e-mo," we sang at the top of our voices as the minibus pulled out of the car park and headed for home.

Final Whistle

I did feel a little gloomy for a few
days after the tournament. It was
nice to be back with my family but
a little dull, too, after all the
drama. Funnily enough, it was Yuri who
stopped me from getting too fed up.
He suggested we should write Uncle's
story down. "War stories are always
popular. We could sell it on eBay
afterwards. I'll do the illustrations,
you can do the writing," he decided.

That weekend Tato took us to
the library to check the facts in
books and on the Internet. Yuri was
delighted to discover that Uncle's
story was known as the Match of Death.
"There's the title, right there," he
said, and he got out his red felt-
tip to draw blood dripping from
the lettering. I am afraid he has a
ghoulish streak.

Writing kept me very occupied.
"You know something?" I said to Yuri
one afternoon when we were halfway
through. "I reckon Uncle is a hero,
too. Living through all that."

We both glanced across at him
sleeping peacefully in his armchair.

"You're right," Yuri said quietly.
"He is."

It took us until the end of the
summer holidays to finish our booklet.
I wrote two versions: one in English
and one in Ukrainian. Mama and Tato
said it was an excellent piece of work
and they had copies made. Yuri didn't
put his copy on eBay, thank goodness.
He took it into school to show his new
teacher instead.

I keep my copy in a secret location,
together with my medal from the
tournament. I suppose I could have put

Jenny-Jane's boots there too, as they are as much of a memento as the medal, but I need those to play in.

It is Jenny-Jane's turn to tell you what happens next with the Parrs. She is going to cover the start of the new season. Please don't be discouraged if she comes across as a little bit blunt at times. She has a big heart underneath – and it is not made of cabbage!

Warm wishes to you all,
Nika Kozak

Acknowledgements

The story Nika's uncle told her about FC Start really happened, but it wasn't until many years later that it became known as the *Match of Death*. There are many Internet accounts of the match, but the two sources I found most helpful were James Riordan's children's book *Match of Death*, published by OUP in 2002; and for adults, Andy Dougan's non-fiction *Dynamo: Defending the Honour of Kiev,* published by Fourth Estate in 2001.

I'd also like to thank Bohdan Drapan, Vera Drapan, Michael Drapan, Lily Hyde and Oleksandr Baranovskyi for their help with the Ukrainian language, and Tom of the Easter and Spring Festival of Football for his useful information about tournaments.

Helena Pielichaty, 2009